"Turn my eyes away from worthless things"
—Psalm 119:37

ZONDERKIDZ

The Berenstain Bears'™ Storybook Collection
Copyright © 2010 by Berenstain Publishing, Inc.
Illustrations © 2010 by Berenstain Publishing, Inc.

Requests for information should be addressed to:

Zondervan, 3900 Sparks Dr., Grand Rapids, Michigan 49546

ISBN 978-0-310-62129-4 (hardcover)

Trouble With Things ISBN 9780310720911
Get Involved ISBN 9780310720904
God Loves You ISBN 9780310712503
Say Their Prayers ISBN 9780310712466
Give Thanks ISBN 9780310712510

Printed in China

5 BOOKS IN 1

Living Lights™

The Berenstain Bears.

Storybook Collection

written by
Jan & Mike Berenstain

The Berenstain Bears®

and the Trouble with THINGS

written by
Jan & Mike Berenstain

Living Lights™

ZONDERkidz

Like most cubs their age, Brother and Sister had a lot of things—things like toys, games, books, puzzles, bikes, skates, soccer balls, a deluxe swing set, a super-bounce trampoline, seventeen Bearbie dolls, the complete Space Grizzlies video library, and much, much more.

But, even though they had all these things, there were plenty of others they would like to have too.

One morning, Brother and Sister noticed Mama getting ready to go out.

"Where are you going, Mama?" Sister asked.

"To the Bear Country Mall," said Mama. "We need new sheets and pillowcases. Our old ones are almost worn out."

"Can we come?" Brother and Sister asked. "There are lots of things we need at the mall too."

"Well ..." said Mama. She wasn't so sure there was anything the cubs really needed. They already had so much. But Papa chimed in as well.

"Let's all go," he said. "I'd like to look at some new fishing gear."

Mama wasn't so sure that Papa really needed new fishing gear, either. But they collected Honey and piled into the car for a trip to the mall.

The Bear Country Mall was humongous. It looked like a giant castle with towers and flags flying. And its parking lot was humongous, too.

The Bear family had to park far away
and take a long hike to the entrance.

Inside the mall, they joined huge crowds of bears
all busily shopping for *things*.

First, they stopped at a store for the sheets and pillowcases
that Mama needed. Brother and Sister were bored.

"Can we go to the toy store?" they asked.

"We'll see," said Mama.

Next, they went to a store for the fishing gear that Papa wanted.
He looked greedily at all the shiny rods, reels, and lures.

He bought himself a new
salmon reel. Brother and
Sister were still bored.

"Can we go to the toy store now?"
they asked.
"We'll see," said Papa.

Salmon
Reel

As they walked through the mall, they passed near the toy store.

"Look!" said Brother and Sister. "We see the toy store! Can we go in? Please? Please? Pretty please?"

Papa and Mama looked at each other and shrugged.
"Well, why not?" they said.
Mama and Papa quickly found out why not.

As soon as they were inside the toy store, Brother and Sister began to ask for things, all kinds of things. Brother asked for a Space Grizzlies play set.

Sister asked for a pink Bearbie dream house with matching pink sports car and pink swimming pool.

And they both asked for new skateboards, new video games, new puzzles, new craft kits, new rollerblades, new minibikes, new baseball gloves, new hockey sticks, and anything else they could think of.

Mama and Papa Bear were not pleased.

"I am shocked ... shocked by how greedy you are!" said Papa, holding his new fishing reel behind his back.

"Well," Mama said in his ear, "maybe we shouldn't be so shocked. After all, we're the ones who gave them all their things to begin with."

"Hmmm," said Papa.
"I guess you're right.
What should we do?"

"I have an idea,"
said Mama. "Let's
stop by the mall's
bookstore."

In the bookstore, Mama picked out a book.

"This is just what we need," she said, opening it. It was a storybook Bible.

She showed the cubs a picture of a king wearing a golden crown and rich robes. He was seated in a garden. All around were beautiful flowers. The colors of the flowers were even brighter than the king's crown and robes.

"Who's that guy?" asked Brother.
"That's King Solomon," said Mama.
"Now listen."

She read:

"See how the flowers of the field grow. They do not labor or spin. Yet I tell you that not even Solomon in all his splendor was dressed like one of these."

"Huh?" said Sister.
"What's that mean?" asked Brother.

"It means," explained Papa, "nothing that a king with all his money can buy is as beautiful as the simple flowers God creates."

"Oh," said Brother and Sister, thinking that over.

"Well," said Mama, "it's time we were getting home."

Soon, they were driving through the
beautiful spring countryside.

"Stop!" said Sister.

"What's the matter?" asked Mama.

"Look at all the flowers," said Sister.

They were passing through
a field of bright yellow flowers.

"Can we stop to pick some?"
Sister asked.

The whole family gathered big armfuls of lovely, fragrant wildflowers. Sister sniffed them deeply.

"I guess these flowers really are more beautiful than King Solly-Man in all his splendor," she said.

"That's 'King Solomon,' dear," said Mama. "But you are right. The things God gives us are much better than anything we can buy."

"What sort of things?" asked Brother.

"Things like the warm sun in the day and the bright moon and twinkling stars at night," said Papa.

"Things like the fresh air we breathe and the cool water we drink," added Mama.

"What about the birds in
the sky and the fish in the sea?"
asked Sister.

"And clouds and rainbows
and rain and snow!" put in Brother.

"Snow!" yelled Honey.
"Well, not today,
Honey," laughed Papa.

The Bear family got back in their car and drove on. As they came to the top of the hill, they could see their tree house home in the valley below, lit up by the golden sunset.

"But one of the best things of all, in God's whole wide world," said Papa, "is our own home, sweet tree."

"And," added Mama, "our own sweet family to go inside."

The Berenstain Bears®

Get Involved

written by
Jan & Mike Berenstain

ZONDERkidz

Living Lights™

Brother and Sister Bear belonged to the Cub Club at the Chapel in the Woods. Preacher Brown was their leader. They did lots of fun things together. They went on picnics,

played baseball

and basketball,

sang in the chorus,
    put on plays, painted
        pictures of Bible stories,

and put up decorations in the
chapel at Christmastime.

But the Cub Club was about
much more than just doing fun
things.

The real purpose of the club was to help others. There was always something that needed to be done around Bear Country. Sometimes it was cleaning up the Beartown playground.

Sometimes it was bringing food to bears who couldn't get out and about.

Sometimes it was even fixing up old houses for folks who couldn't fix them up themselves.

Brother and Sister liked to be helpful. It made them feel good deep down inside. Preacher Brown explained that it was always a good thing to help those in need.

"As the Bible says," he told them, "'Whoever is kind to the needy honors God.'"

So the Cub Club went right on helping others all over Bear Country.

Little did they know that very soon their help would be truly needed indeed!

One morning at breakfast, Papa Bear was reading the weather forecast.

"Says here it will rain for the next two days," he said. "Rain, rain, and more rain!"

"Oh, dear," said Mama. "I was planning to do laundry and air it out on the line. It will have to wait."

Brother and Sister didn't pay much attention. A little rain didn't seem to be anything to get very excited about.

On the way to school, Brother and Sister noticed the sky growing very dark.

By the time they reached school, it was starting to drizzle.

Through the morning, it rained
harder and harder. It rained so hard that
recess was cancelled and they had
a study period instead.

"Phooey on rain!" muttered Brother.

"Rain, rain, go away," recited Sister.
"Come again some other day."

But the rain paid no
attention. It came pouring
down harder than ever.

"I think you made it
worse," said Brother.

When school let out, the cubs splashed their way home through the puddles. But then they heard a car coming down the road. It was Mama. She was coming to pick them up.

"Thanks, Mama," said the cubs. "We were getting soaked!"

Back home, Papa had a fire going in the fireplace, and Mama spread their wet clothes out to dry. Brother and Sister played with Honey in front of the cozy fire.

"This rain is getting serious," said Papa. "There could be flooding along the river."

"Oh, dear!" said Mama. "That's where Uncle Ned, Aunt Min, and Cousin Fred live. I do hope they don't get flooded out."

Brother and Sister pricked up their ears. What would it mean if Cousin Fred's family got "flooded out"?

At bedtime, Brother and Sister could hear the wind howling and the rain beating against the windows. It was a little spooky, but they snuggled down under the covers and soon drifted off to sleep.

They dreamed about
rushing streams

and roaring waterfalls.

It was still raining when they woke up the next morning.

"Wow!" said Brother, pressing against the windowpane. "Look at it coming down!"

As Brother and Sister went downstairs, they heard Papa on the phone.

"Don't worry," he said. "I'll be right over!"

"Over where?" asked Mama.

"That was Preacher Brown," said Papa, getting his coat and hat. "The river is rising fast, and we'll need to get everyone out of their houses down there. We're meeting at the chapel."

"We'll all come with you," said Mama. "There'll be plenty for everyone to do."

Brother and Sister were excited. They had never been part of a rescue mission before.

At the Chapel in the Woods, bears were gathering from all over. Their cars were loaded with shovels and buckets, bundles of blankets, and boxes of food. Grizzly Gus had a load of sandbags in his truck.

Preacher Brown saw Brother, Sister, and some of the other cubs. "I want all you Cub Club members to go along with your dads and help out," he told them. "This is what the Cub Club is all about!"

"Yes, sir!" they said. They were glad to be going. And Brother and Sister especially wanted to make sure Cousin Fred was all right.

The cars drove through the storm, down to the river.

"We're just in time," said Papa. "The water is nearly up to the houses."

An angry river was swirling over its banks and lapping toward the houses.

"Look! There's Cousin Fred!" said Sister.

Cousin Fred, with Uncle Ned and Aunt Min, was leaning out of an upstairs window and waving.

The bears all set to work piling up sandbags and digging ditches to keep the water away from the houses. Brother, Sister, Cousin Fred, and the rest of the Cub Club joined in. They dug and dug and dug until they were cold, wet, and tired.

Then everyone drove back to the chapel to warm up, dry off, and get something to eat.

Preacher Brown's wife, along with Mama and the other moms, had soup and sandwiches ready for all those cold, wet bears. They wrapped them in dry blankets and settled them down in the chapel's pews. Miz McGrizz sat at the organ to give them a little music.

"I'm so glad you're all right!" said Mama to Uncle Ned, Aunt Min, and Cousin Fred, giving them big hugs and kisses.

Preacher Brown got up in the pulpit, opened the Bible, and started to read: "The floodgates of the heavens were opened. And rain fell on the earth ... The waters flooded the earth ..."

Sister noticed a bright light coming through the chapel windows.

"Look!" she said. "The rain is stopping, and the sun is coming out!"

"The rain had stopped falling from the sky," read Preacher Brown.

"And there's a rainbow!" said Brother.

"I have set my rainbow in the clouds, ..." Preacher Brown read, and closed the Bible.

"With God's help, we are all safe and sound," said Preacher Brown. "Thanks to everyone for pitching in and helping out. I particularly want to thank our youngest helpers, the members of the Cub Club."

All the bears clapped for Brother, Sister, Cousin Fred, and the Cub Club. They had been there to help others when their help was truly needed.

The Berenstain Bears
God Loves You!

by Stan and Jan Berenstain
with Mike Berenstain

ZONDERkidz

The first week of school was a busy time for Brother and Sister Bear. It was a time to see old friends, meet new teachers, get their first homework assignments, and sign up for after-school activities.

Sister decided to try out for the big school show. This year it was *The Music Bear*. Sister thought she would be perfect in a leading role. She liked to sing "I Feel Pretty" from *Bearside Story* at home. Mama and Papa always said she was very good.

But there would be a lot of other girls trying out for the show too. Babs Bruno had a very fine voice, and there was Queenie McBear, of course. She thought she was the best singer in the school, and all her friends agreed with her.

THE
MUSIC BEAR
Tryouts

Sister

Brother Bear was trying out too, but not for the school show. He wanted to be on the school basketball team. He was pretty sure he could make it. He had been practicing dribbling and layups in the driveway at home. He played 21 with Papa after supper and always beat him.

Basketball Tryouts

Brother Be

The tryouts for the school play and basketball team were on the same day. After school, Brother went down to the gym and got into a basketball uniform. He and the other boys charged out onto the court and started warming up.

Sister joined a long line of cubs in the
auditorium. Teacher Jane called them up on
the stage one by one to sing a song. Babs
sang "Memory," and she was very good. But
Queenie made a mess of "Tomorrow"! She had
a hard time hitting all the high notes. In spite of
that, all her friends clapped and cheered, and
Queenie took a few bows. Sister glanced over
at Teacher Jane. She didn't look too impressed.

When it was Sister's turn, she sang "I Feel
Pretty" just like she did at home for Mama
and Papa.

In the gym, Brother was puffing and panting away, trying hard to look good. One after another, the boys dribbled, passed, shot layups, and took foul shots while Coach Grizzmeyer looked on and checked off names on a clipboard. You couldn't tell anything by watching him. His face never changed—never a smile, never a frown, not even a wink. The cubs called him Old Stoneface.

Finally, he said, "Okay, men! That's enough! The roster will be posted on the bulletin board outside my office tomorrow."

On his way back to the locker room, Brother couldn't resist stopping to ask, "Coach, do you think I have a shot at making the team?"

Coach Grizzmeyer just shrugged and said, "We'll see, son."

In the auditorium, the auditions for the school show were winding up. Teacher Jane smiled a lot more than Coach Grizzmeyer, but she wasn't giving anything away, either.

"That's all for today, everyone!" she said. "I'll post my choices for the entire cast tomorrow on the bulletin board outside my room."

As Sister left, she couldn't resist stopping to ask, "Teacher Jane, do you think I have a chance of getting one of the main parts?"

But Teacher Jane just smiled and said, "We'll see, my dear."

Sister joined up with Brother as he walked home from school.

"Well, how do you think it went?" asked Sister. "Do you think you made the team?"

"Yeah, I think so!" said Brother hopefully. He really felt he had done well. He knew he was still a little short to be playing on the school team. But he hoped his skills and his hustle would make up for that.

"What about you?" Brother asked. "How did the auditions go?"

"Great, I think," said Sister.

"What did Teacher Jane think?" Brother asked.

"I don't know," said Sister thoughtfully. "She didn't say anything. She just smiled at everybody."

"At least she smiled. Old Stoneface never smiles!"

Sister laughed as they reached their tree house and climbed the steps.

"Oh, well!" she said, shrugging. "We'll find out how we did tomorrow."

And they did …

The next morning, both Brother and Sister rushed downstairs, gobbled their breakfasts, waved a quick good-bye to Mama and Papa, and got to school faster than they ever had before. They couldn't wait to see how they had done.

Brother rushed to Coach Grizzmeyer's office while Sister scurried to Teacher Jane's room. There were crowds of cubs gathered around the bulletin boards. Brother and Sister struggled to get up close.

Basketball
TEAM
LINEUP

Barry Bruin
Cousin Fred
Too-Tall Grizzly
Bob Bruno
Vinnie Bearkin
Chuck Ursullini
Sam Honeytree
Ralph O' Grizz
Lou Bearens
Chuck
Sam Honey
Ralph O' Griz
Lou Bearens
Brother Bear: Team Manager

Brother glanced quickly down the list of names. There was his, right at the bottom. At first, he felt a rush of relief. But then, he noticed what it said next to his name: Team Manager.

Team manager! TEAM MANAGER? The team manager just picked up basketballs and made sure everybody got on the bus on time. That's not what he wanted to do! He wanted to play; he wanted to shoot and dribble and dunk. He wanted to be a big star!

Crushed, he slunk down the hallway to his classroom.

THE MUSIC BEAR CAST

Ferdy Factual: Henry Hill
Babs Bruno: Marian
Ziggy Grizowsky: The Mayor
Queenie McBear: Mrs. Paroo
Harry Bearkis: Eddie
Bonnie Brown: Eulalie
Anna Grizzle: Gracie
Ron Ursowitz: Mr. Washburn
Sister Bear: Stage Manager

Outside Teacher Jane's room, Sister quickly looked over the cast. At first, she didn't see her name at all. Then she spotted it, right at the bottom.

Sister Bear: Stage Manager.

Stage manager! STAGE MANAGER? All the stage manager did was put away the props and make sure everybody got onstage on time. She didn't want to be stage manager. She wanted to act; she wanted to sing and dance and take bows. She wanted to be a big star!

Miserably, Sister trudged down the hall to her classroom.

When school let out that afternoon, Brother and Sister were both feeling very sorry for themselves. Even the weather seemed to be against them. Slowly, they climbed the front steps of the tree house.

Wearily, they plopped themselves down on the sofa in the living room. It seemed like the dark rain clouds outside had followed them in and were hanging over them.

"Whatever is the matter?" asked Mama.

"Yes," said Papa. "You both look like you are about to get a tooth drilled."

Brother and Sister sighed.

"Oh, we had a rough day at school," said Brother. "I didn't make the school basketball team."

"And I didn't get a part in the school show," added Sister, putting her chin in her hands.

"Oh, dear!" said Papa, concerned. "What a shame!"

"How disappointing!" said Mama. "Didn't Coach Grizzmeyer or Teacher Jane give you anything to do at all?"

"Well," said Brother, "they did give us something to do. I'm the team manager."

"And I'm the stage manager," said Sister. "But I don't want to do that! I want to be in the show!"

"And I want to be on the team!" said Brother.

"Well," said Mama, "I guess not everybody can be a star."

"But don't you think I deserve to be in the show?" asked Sister.

"Of course you do!" said Mama, giving her a hug. "You're a wonderful singer!"

"And don't you think I deserve to be on the team?" asked Brother.

"Of course you do!" said Papa, patting him on the shoulder. "You're a terrific basketball player!"

"I guess nobody else thinks so," said Sister gloomily. "I guess nobody at Bear Country School thinks much of us at all!" She heaved an even bigger sigh.

"Well," said Mama, "it's not going to do us any good sitting around here feeling sorry for ourselves. I was just about to go outside to cut some flowers. It's getting chilly at night, and I want to get them in before there's a frost. Why don't we all go out for a little walk?

"But it's raining," protested Brother.

"The rain's stopped," said Papa, looking out the window. Sure enough, the clouds had lifted and the sun was peeking out.

Papa got Honey Bear into her stroller, and they all went outside. Mama stopped to cut some flowers at the back gate. They were very beautiful—big bright yellow, orange, pink, and violet blossoms. Birds were coming out after the rain and were singing in the trees. A big blue butterfly came sailing by and stopped to sip nectar from Mama's flowers. By now, the clouds had all rolled away and the golden sun was shining over the countryside.

"Look!" said Papa. "A rainbow!"

As the rays of the sun shone through the last drops of rain, a beautiful rainbow stretched right across the sky. "Wow!" said Brother. "It's so bright!"

"What makes a rainbow?" asked Sister in wonder.

"Well," said Papa, "you see … the light from the sun shines through the raindrops and creates a prismatic thingy, which bounces around from the um … uh …"

Mama interrupted. "The rainbow is a gift from God. It's a sign that the rain is past and the sun has come to warm the earth again. God puts the rainbow in the sky as a beautiful sign of his love for all the earth and all the creatures that he has made."

"Even us?" asked Brother.

"Of course!" said Papa. "God loves everybody!"

"What about wasps?" asked Sister. A wasp had stung her in the school yard a few days ago, and she was very afraid of them.

"Well ... yes," said Papa, shooing one away that was buzzing around Mama's flowers. "God loves all his creation!"

"Does he love us even when we're bad?" wondered Brother, a little puzzled.

"Well ..." said Papa.

"What about when we're really, really bad?" asked Sister. "Like when Brother and I got into a fight and wouldn't speak to each other for a week?"

"Um ..." said Papa.

"Or that time Too-Tall Grizzly and his gang dared me to steal Farmer Ben's watermelon?" asked Brother.

"Uh ..." said Papa.

"Or when we watch too much TV?" put in Sister. "Or when I bite my nails? Or when we don't do our homework? Or when—"

"YES!" Mama broke in, suddenly. "He does!"

They all looked at her in surprise.

"You see," she explained patiently, "God wants us to be good. But he doesn't love us because we're good or bad. God loves us because he made us. It's a little bit like how mothers and fathers love their children."

"Oh," said Sister. "Like how you still love us even when we do things we're not supposed to?"

"That's right," said Papa. "Of course, we're disappointed when you misbehave. But we still love you! We even love you when you don't make the basketball team or get a part in the school show! And we're proud of you because your coach and teacher trusted you to be managers—special jobs for the most responsible cubs."

Brother and Sister smiled. They were beginning to feel slightly better about that little problem.

By now they had made their way down the lane to a spot that overlooked Farmer Ben's farm. It was a lovely scene. The cows were coming in from the pasture, the ducks were swimming in the pond, bees were buzzing around their hives, and the sun was setting behind the trees.

As the sky grew darker, they noticed a tiny point of light in the western sky.

"What's that?" wondered Brother.

"That's the evening star," said Papa. "It comes out just after sunset."

"Is that another sign of God's love?" asked Sister.

"Yes, dear," said Mama, giving her a hug. "It surely is!"

And, hand in hand, the Bear family turned for home and their evening meal.

The Berenstain Bears.
Say Their Prayers

Created by Stan and Jan Berenstain
Written by Mike Berenstain

ZONDERkidz

It was bedtime in the Bear family's tree house—bedtime after a long, busy day. Little Honey Bear was already asleep in her crib. Brother and Sister were ready for bed too. They were bathed and they had their pajamas on. Mama and Papa were done reading them their bedtime stories. But there was one last thing to do before they went to sleep. It was time for Brother and Sister to kneel down beside their bunk bed and say their prayers.

Some evenings, they added a few more blessings like "bless our friends Lizzy and Barry" or "bless Teacher Jane and Teacher Bob." But when they started adding "bless Mayor Honeypot and Police Chief Bruno," Mama and Papa decided to draw the line. Mama and Papa were falling asleep before the cubs' prayers were over.

Tonight when Mama and Papa were giving the cubs their goodnight kisses, Brother asked a question. It was a question he had been thinking about for awhile.

"Mama," he said. "Why do we say prayers before we go to sleep? I was at Barry Bruin's house for a sleepover last week, and he doesn't say prayers at all."

"Some people just don't believe in saying prayers," said Mama. "But we pray at night so we can thank God for the blessings of the day."

"Do you and Papa always say your prayers before you go to sleep?" asked Sister, half asleep in the upper bunk.

"Not exactly …" said Mama. These days Mama and Papa were so tired at bedtime that they just flopped down and were snoring almost before their heads hit the pillow. "But I think it would be a good idea if we got in the habit again." Mamma nudged Papa. "Don't you agree, Papa?"

"Huh?" he said, trying to stay awake. "Oh, right! Absolutely!"

"Good night now," said Mama. "Sweet dreams."

"Hmmm ..." thought Brother, as he drifted off in the sleepy darkness. Mama's answer was okay. But he still had a few questions.

The next morning, Brother and Sister were up bright and early. It was Saturday and they had a Little League game. Their team was called the Sharks. They had a cool logo on their shirts—a big shark mouth full of sharp teeth.

"I feel hot today!" said Sister, tying her shoes. "I feel a whole lot of hits and stolen bases coming on!"

"Oh, yeah?" snorted Brother. "What about home runs? I guess I'll have to take care of that department!"

"Sure!" said Sister, punching him in the arm. "Brother Bear, the Home-Run King!" She ran, laughing, out of the room with Brother Bear chasing her. Sister and Brother liked playing on the same team. But sometimes they got just a little too competitive.

After breakfast, the whole family headed down to the ball field. Brother and Sister had practice before the game. It was Mama and Papa's turn to help with the snack bar. Papa was going to cook the hamburgers and hot dogs on the grill. Mama was going to sell candy and popcorn. Even Honey Bear would help out. It was her job to eat the leftover cotton candy. Papa soon had the grill behind the snack bar fired up. Mama opened up the candy stand, and Honey Bear started getting into the cotton candy.

The team ran out on the field for practice. Brother was playing shortstop, and Sister was at second base. Up on the mound, Cousin Fred would handle the pitching. Fred was a solid pitcher. But he had been struggling of late. His last two games were pretty shaky.

Today, they were up against the Pumas. The Pumas' uniforms weren't quite as cool as the Sharks'. But the Pumas were one of the best teams in the league. The Sharks would have their work cut out for them.

Since the Sharks were the home team, the Pumas were up first. Their lead-off batter was a big, powerful cub about twice Brother's size. He was twirling six bats around his head in the warm-up circle as if they were a bunch of twigs.

"Uh-oh!" said Brother. "Look who it is!"

Sister gulped. It was the Beast—the Pumas' best player. He could hit and field and pitch. They didn't know his real name. They just called him the Beast.

Brother glanced over at Fred on the mound. He had noticed too. He was taking off his hat to wipe his forehead. He looked pretty nervous out there.

"Play ball!" called the ump, and the game was on.

The Beast picked out a bat from his bunch and stepped into the batter's box. He took some warm-up swings and pounded his bat on the plate. He glared at Fred on the mound.

Brother noticed that Fred wasn't glaring back. In fact, he was standing quite still, his head bowed and his hands folded. It looked like his eyes were closed, and his lips seemed to be moving.

"Psst, Fred!" called Brother. "What's up?"

But Fred didn't answer. He straightened up, took a deep breath, and went into his windup. He fired a fast ball. There was a *swish* and a *thump*! The Beast had missed!

"Stee-rike one!" called the ump.

"Way to go, Freddy baby!" yelled Brother. "That's the way to pitch 'em in there! Just two more like that! You can do it!"

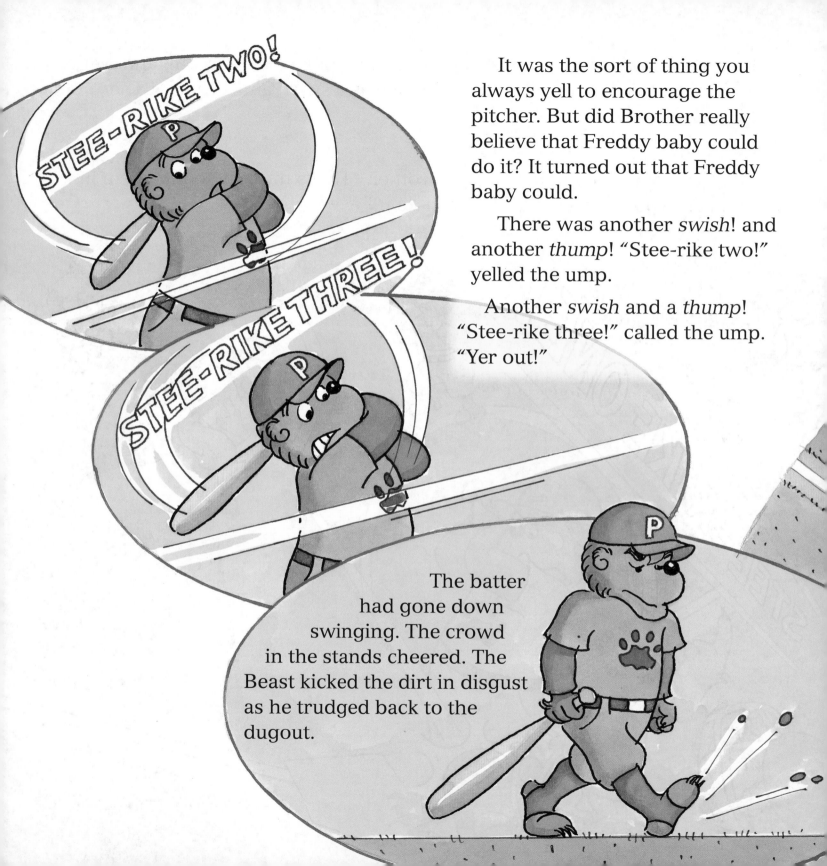

It was the sort of thing you always yell to encourage the pitcher. But did Brother really believe that Freddy baby could do it? It turned out that Freddy baby could.

There was another *swish!* and another *thump!* "Stee-rike two!" yelled the ump.

Another *swish* and a *thump!* "Stee-rike three!" called the ump. "Yer out!"

The batter had gone down swinging. The crowd in the stands cheered. The Beast kicked the dirt in disgust as he trudged back to the dugout.

Fred didn't look nervous anymore. Now it was the batter's turn to look nervous. Fred threw six more fast balls to two more batters. There were six *swishes* and six *thumps*. Cousin Fred had struck out the side!

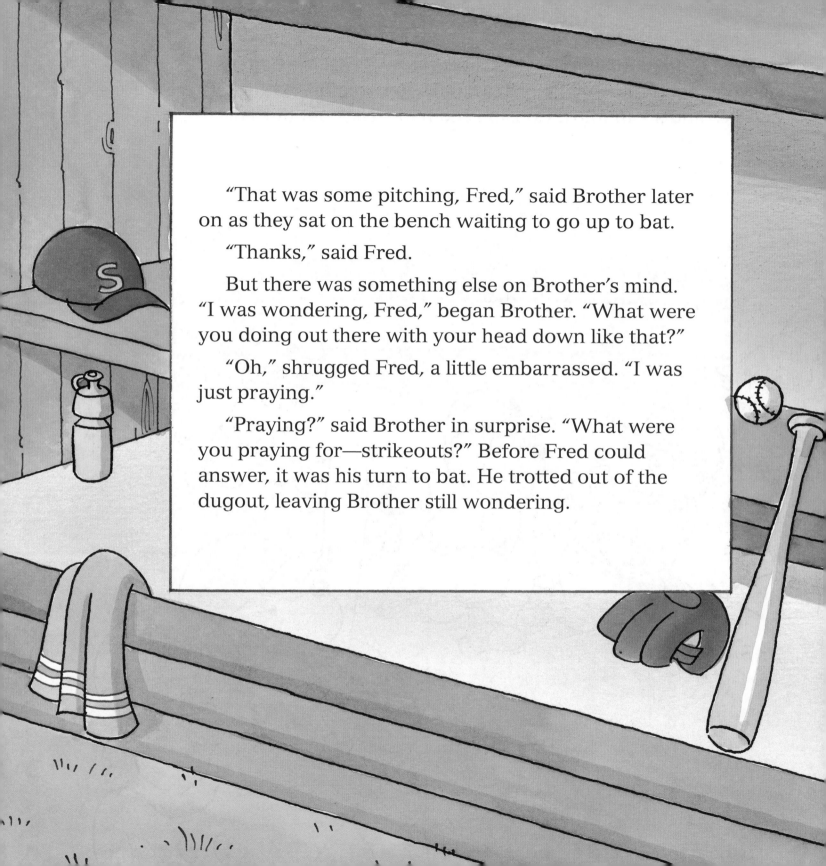

"That was some pitching, Fred," said Brother later on as they sat on the bench waiting to go up to bat.

"Thanks," said Fred.

But there was something else on Brother's mind. "I was wondering, Fred," began Brother. "What were you doing out there with your head down like that?"

"Oh," shrugged Fred, a little embarrassed. "I was just praying."

"Praying?" said Brother in surprise. "What were you praying for—strikeouts?" Before Fred could answer, it was his turn to bat. He trotted out of the dugout, leaving Brother still wondering.

BATTING ORDER
1. Barry Bruin 3B
2. Anna Grizzly LF
3. Cousin Fred P
4. Sister Bear 2B
5. Brother Bear SS
6. Lizzy Bruin RF
7. Millie Bruno CF
8. Harry McBear 1B
9. Bill Grizzwold C

By the end of the game, Papa had cooked thirty-three hamburgers and forty-seven hot dogs; Mama had sold three dozen lollipops and four boxes of chocolate bars; and Honey Bear was very, very sticky.

The Sharks were in a sticky spot too. They were behind by one run with two outs and a man on base. The "man" was Sister. She had gotten to first on a walk and then stolen second—she was a feisty little player. Now it was Brother's turn to bat. If he could get a hit, the Sharks might tie it. If he got a home run, they would win.

The Pumas' pitcher was none other than the Beast. As he walked to the plate, Brother felt a little sick. Talk about pressure!

Before he stepped into the batter's box, Brother decided to do something he had never done in a baseball game. He bowed his head, closed his eyes, and said a prayer. "Dear Lord," he prayed. "Please let me get a hit."

Feeling a little more confident, Brother stepped up to the plate. The Beast wound up and let it fly. Brother didn't even see it.

"Stee-rike one!" called the ump.

Brother gripped the bat tighter. He'd get the next one. Another scorcher screamed past.

"Stee-rike two!" called the ump.

Brother clenched his teeth. He was definitely not going to let this next pitch get past him. The Beast wound up, the ball flew, and Brother swung—hard!

Swish!—Thump! "Stee-rike three!" bawled the ump. "Yer out!"

The game was over. The Sharks had lost, and Brother had struck out!

"Way to go, Home-Run King!" shouted Sister in disgust. She was angry that all her efforts to get on base had gone to waste. Brother trudged back to the dugout, his head hung low. He had never felt so awful in his life!

Later, as he packed up his things, he found Fred standing next to him. "Don't let it get to you, Brother," said Fred. "That was a tough game. The Pumas are a good team."

"Yeah," agreed Brother. "I tried everything. I even tried praying like you did when you struck out the Beast. But it didn't work for me."

"Really?" said Fred. "What did you pray for?"

"I prayed for a hit, naturally," said Brother.

"Oh," said Fred, rubbing his chin. "I see."

"Why?" asked Brother. "What did you pray for?"

"I just prayed that I wouldn't get too scared," said Fred simply.

Brother blinked at him. "I guess your prayer was answered!"

"Prayers are always answered," said Fred. "Sometimes, we just don't get the answer we expect. Say," he added, sniffing the air. "Do you smell something burning?"

That's when they noticed the column of thick black smoke rising from behind the stands. "The snack bar!" they both yelled, and ran for it.

The smoke was coming from a batch of burning hot dogs on the grill. Papa was covered with soot and was trying to put the fire out with his hat. Mama came running up with a fire extinguisher. A few good squirts and the flames were under control. Honey Bear was laughing and clapping.

"Boy!" coughed Fred, waving the smoke away. "Maybe we should have prayed for rain!"

That evening at bedtime, Brother and Sister knelt down beside their bunk bed to say their prayers. Tonight, they felt like a nice long one:

"Bless Mama, bless Papa, bless Honey Bear, bless Grizzly Gramps, bless Grizzly Gran, bless Cousin Fred, Uncle Willie, and Aunt Min. Bless our friends Lizzie and Barry, and bless Teacher Bob, and ..."

When they were finished, Brother and Sister woke Mama and Papa up and climbed into bed. Mama and Papa kissed them goodnight, turned out the light, and went downstairs.

As Brother lay drowsily in his bed, he started thinking over the day's baseball game. If only he had been able to get that hit … or even a home run!

"That was a tough game today, wasn't it?" he said to Sister up on the top bunk.

"Yeah," answered Sister. "Tough on you, Mr. Strike-Out King."

"What's that supposed to mean?" said Brother, glaring up at the bottom of her bunk. "I played my best! A strike out like that could happen to anybody!"

But Sister didn't answer. She was fast asleep. Brother rolled over and ground his teeth. Sometimes Sister Bear made him so angry he could just … But then he thought of something. He thought of another prayer.

"Dear God," he prayed. "Please help me out with my little sister!" And to his surprise, he found his prayer had been answered. He didn't feel angry anymore.

"Thanks for the help up there!" he said.
And with a sigh, he fell asleep.

The Berenstain Bears

Give Thanks

written by Jan and Mike Berenstain

ZONDERkidz

It was autumn in Bear Country, and the sights and the sounds of the season were all around. The leaves on the trees were turning orange, red, and gold. There was a nip in the air, and the sky was a brilliant blue. Flocks of geese flew overhead honking their way south for the winter. Out in his cornfield, Farmer Ben was up on his big red tractor harvesting his crop.

Papa, Brother, and Sister Bear waved to him as they drove up the long drive to the farm. Papa was delivering some new furniture for Mrs. Ben. It was a fine new kitchen table and chairs.

Ben climbed down from his tractor and went to meet them at the farmhouse. Papa and the cubs unloaded the table and chairs and carried them inside. Mrs. Ben was pleased.

"My, don't they look nice!" she said. "It brightens the place up a bit. They do make my curtains look a mite shabby, though. I guess it's time I made some new ones."

"Thank you, Papa Bear," said Ben, shaking hands. "A job well done! Now, about our little deal ..."

The cubs wondered what "deal" Ben was talking about.

"I told you that you could have the pick of my produce in payment for the furniture," said Ben.

"That's right, Ben," said Papa as he nodded. "I was thinking of a few cases of your extra-special, grade-A, apple-blossom honey." Papa licked his lips just thinking about all that delicious honey.

"That's fine," agreed Ben. "You're welcome to it. And I have something else behind the barn that I think might interest you."

"Meet Squanto," said Ben, "my tom turkey. Isn't he a beaut?" Squanto was, indeed, a magnificent bird. He was enormous with a huge fanned tail and glowing colors of black, red, and gold.

"Wow!" said Papa, impressed. "That's some turkey!"

"He's beautiful!" said Sister. "But why is he called 'Squanto'?"

"That was the name of the Native Bear who helped the Pilgrims plant their corn when they settled in their new home," explained Ben. "Squanto celebrated the first Thanksgiving with them after their harvest. I couldn't think of a better name for a turkey."

"He sure is a fine bird," said Papa. "But what's he got to do with my furniture?"

"He's yours if you want him," said Ben. "He'll make you the best Thanksgiving dinner in all Bear Country."

Papa's eyes brightened. "Roast turkey—mmm-*mmm*!"

"Thanksgiving dinner?" said Sister, getting upset. "But that means ..."

"Now don't you fret, Sister Bear," soothed Ben. "Squanto can stay here till Thanksgiving. I'll fatten him up and deliver him all ready for your mama to cook on Thanksgiving morning.

"What do you say, Papa? Is it a deal?"

"It's a deal, Ben!" said Papa, and they shook hands on it. Papa was already imagining that mouth-watering Thanksgiving dinner—roast turkey with stuffing, two kinds of potatoes, gravy, green beans, and squash. Then dessert—pumpkin pie with whipped cream, and maybe some ice cream on top. Yum!

But Sister Bear wasn't so sure she liked the sound of all this. She had never met her Thanksgiving dinner before. It made things more personal. And Squanto was such a beautiful bird. She liked him a lot.

"You know, Papa," she said as they drove home, "I don't think having Squanto for Thanksgiving dinner is such a good idea. I think he would make a nice pet."

"A pet?" said Papa in surprise. "Who ever heard of a turkey for a pet?"

"Why not?" asked Sister. "Lots of cubs have unusual pets. Barry Bruin has a raccoon. Lizzie Bruin has a goat. And Too-Tall Grizzly has a snake. Why couldn't I have a turkey?"

Papa thought of that roast turkey Thanksgiving dinner with all the trimmings.

"Turkeys just don't make good pets," he said. "And that's all there is to it!"

But Sister still didn't like the idea of Squanto being a Thanksgiving dinner.

The weeks went past, and the leaves fell from the trees. The wind grew positively chilly, and one day, a few flakes of snow fell. Thanksgiving was drawing near.

Every day, Sister visited Squanto at the farm. He was growing fatter and finer. His feathers were bright and glossy. When he spread his tail, he looked like a big black, red, and gold peacock. But the closer it got to Thanksgiving, the sadder Sister got. She liked Squanto more and more each day.

Mama noticed that Sister was down in the dumps.

"You know, Sister," said Mama, putting her arm around her shoulder, "Papa's right—turkeys don't make very good pets. They aren't like dogs or cats. You can't play with them or run and jump with them. They're really just farm animals."

"I know," Sister sighed. "But I still like Squanto. He's so pretty."

Mama grew thoughtful. She saw that Sister was really serious about this.

"Now, dear, don't worry about it," she said. "Papa and I will talk it over and I'm sure we can work out something."

Sister brightened up. "Really?" she said. "You mean we won't have Squanto for Thanksgiving dinner?"

"We shall see what we shall see," Mama said, smiling. "And, in the meantime, I have a surprise for you. I've been thinking we should make this Thanksgiving into something extra special. Grizzly Gramps and Gran, Uncle Wilbur, Aunt Min, and Cousin Fred will be coming over for dinner. I thought we could put on a show for them."

"A show?" said Sister, looking excited. She loved putting on a show. "What kind of show?"

"I thought the story of the first Thanksgiving would be appropriate," said Mama. "It could tell all about how the Pilgrims and the Native Bears celebrated the first Thanksgiving together hundreds of years ago."

"Neat!" said Sister. "Will we have costumes?"

"Of course," said Mama. "We can make them ourselves. I have lots of old fabric we can use. But we'll need feathers for the Native Bears' headdresses."

"Squanto dropped lots of tail feathers," said Sister. "They're perfect! I've been saving them."

She ran upstairs to get her collection of turkey tail feathers. She brought them down to Mama's sewing room. Mama had the *P* book from the Bear Encyclopedia open to *Pilgrims* so she could see what their clothes looked like.

"You're right, dear," said Mama, taking the feathers. "These are perfect.

But do you know what else we'll need?"

Sister shook her head.

"We'll need a script for the play," said Mama. "Why don't you write one?"

"Me?"

"Certainly," said Mama, getting out her fabric and spreading it out. "You know the story of the first Thanksgiving, don't you?"

"I guess so," said Sister. She had heard about it in school over and over again every November. She should know it pretty well by now.

"Well, there you are," mumbled Mama, her mouth full of pins as she started work.

So, Sister got out a pad of paper and a pencil and set to work. It was hard. She had never written a play before. She asked Brother for help. Sister wrote the script, and Brother copied the parts for each player. Sister was so busy working on the play that she forgot all about Squanto the turkey for a while.

When Thanksgiving Day finally arrived, everything was ready. The script was written and copied, Mama had sewn beautiful Pilgrim and Native Bear costumes, and the tree house was full of the wonderful smells of Thanksgiving dinner.

Around two o'clock, Grizzly Gramps and Gran, Uncle Wilbur, Aunt Min, and Cousin Fred arrived. Sister and Brother grabbed Fred and took him up to their room to rehearse. Fred had a part in the play too.

An hour later, just before dinnertime, Sister made an appearance on the landing of the stairs. She was dressed as a Pilgrim maiden.

"May I have your attention, please?" she called.
The grown-ups all turned toward her. "Oh, isn't she darling!" said Aunt Min. Sister did look very cute in her Pilgrim maiden hat.

"We will now present *The Story of the First Thanksgiving!*" she announced. The grown-ups all applauded and found their seats to watch the play.

All the grown-ups clapped and stamped and whistled. It was a big hit! Aunt Min wiped her eyes. "They're all so darling!" she sniffed.

Mama rang a bell in the doorway. "Dinnertime!" she called.

"Yea!" cried the cubs as they ran for the dining room. But then, Sister stopped short.

"Oh, no!" she said. "What about my turkey, Squanto? I forgot all about him! What happened to Squanto?"

"Don't worry, Sister," said Papa, leading her to the window. "Squanto is safe and sound. I decided that turkeys do make good pets after all!"

And there, in his own brand-new pen in the Bears' own backyard, was Squanto. His tail was spread proudly, and he looked very pleased with himself.

"Oh, Squanto!" said Sister, very happy. "Welcome to your new home!"

The Bear family all gathered around the dining table. Everything was just as Papa had imagined it—two kinds of potatoes, stuffing and gravy, corn on the cob and corn muffins, green beans, pumpkin pie with whipped cream, and ice cream too. But, in the center of the table, instead of a roast turkey, there was a magnificent honey-baked salmon.

"MMM-*MMM!*" said all the bears.

Then it was time to say grace. The Bear family held hands and bowed their heads. Grizzly Gramps, as the eldest of the clan, said the prayer.

"Dear Lord, we give thanks for all your blessings—for this great feast that you have provided, for the warm homes that give us shelter, for the love of our family that surrounds us today, and for all the beauties of the earth that you in your great love and wisdom have created. Amen!"

"Amen!" everyone said, picking up their knives and forks.

But Sister had something to add.
"And I am especially thankful for my wonderful new pet, Squanto the turkey!"

"AMEN!" everyone said again. And they all laughed.

"Men!" echoed Honey as they dug into that delicious food like a family of hungry bears.

The Berenstain Bears®

and the Trouble with THINGS

Activities and Questions from Brother and Sister Bear

Talk about it:

1. Brother and Sister have a lot of things. Do you have a lot of things? Which ones are the most important to you? How did you decide that? How would you feel if you did not have all of your things?

2. What has God given you? What is your most precious gift from God?

Get out and do it:

1. There are people who have very little. Talk with your family about how you can help someone in your church or community that is less fortunate than you. Work together as a family and do one of the following: have a canned food drive, collect blankets in the winter for the homeless, get others to participate and have a bake sale. Give the proceeds to the poor.

2. Say thank you to God! As a family, pray together, thanking God for all of the gifts he has given you. Thanking him is not only for Thanksgiving time, but for all the time!

The Berenstain Bears®

Activities and Questions from Brother and Sister Bear

Talk about it:

1. What types of things did the Cub Club usually do for the Bear community? Does the youth group or Sunday school at your church do any of the same activities and service projects?

2. Why did many of the bears of Bear Country gather at the Chapel in the Woods?

3. Why do you think Brother and Sister are especially interested in helping out during the big rains?

Get out and do it:

1. As a family, get involved in a community or church project. Help collect food items for a food drive or blankets for a blanket collection. Organize a bake sale, and donate the funds to a local charity or to your church's service organization or mission.

2. Getting involved can be as simple as making cards for neighborhood shut-ins or people from your church that are in the hospital or a nursing home. Gather some of your friends, and make cards or write letters that give encouragement and hope to others.

The Berenstain Bears® God Loves You!

Activities and Questions from Brother and Sister Bear

Talk about it:

1. Why did the director and coach choose Brother and Sister as managers instead of for the parts they wanted?

2. What are some signs of God's love around you right now?

Get out and do it:

1. Draw or paint a beautiful rainbow, flower, or butterfly.

2. Make a photo album of people you love. Add cutouts, stickers, and drawings of hearts, rainbows, and stars to remind you that signs of God's love are everywhere.

3. Count how many times you can bounce a ball without stopping. Try bouncing it different ways and count (with a clap in between, with your other hand, between your legs, etc.).

The Berenstain Bears

Say Their Prayers

Activities and Questions from Brother and Sister Bear

Talk about it:

1. What did Fred mean when he said, "Prayers are always answered. Sometimes we just don't get the answer we expect"?

2. How do you think Brother's prayer at the end of the book helped him with the problem he had with his sister?

Get out and do it:

1. Design a cool shirt for a sports team called the Bears.

2. Visit a park with a baseball field. Run around the bases. Name something you are good at or thankful for at each base.

3. Make up and memorize a prayer for bedtime. Say it every night before you go to bed.

The Berenstain Bears

Give Thanks

Activities and Questions from Brother and Sister Bear

Talk about it:

1. What are you thankful for?

2. What words describe Thanksgiving at your house? Try to use all of your senses and feelings.

3. In what ways is a turkey a good pet? What unusual pet would you like?

Get out and do it:

1. Tell, write, or act out a Thanksgiving story.

2. Draw, color, or make a collage of a turkey and its feathers.

3. Walk like a turkey. Walk like another animal someone names.